Stacey and the Boyfriend Trap

Other books by
Ann M. Martin

P.S. Longer Letter Later
(written with Paula Danziger)
Leo the Magnificat
Rachel Parker, Kindergarten Show-off
Eleven Kids, One Summer
Ma and Pa Dracula
Yours Turly, Shirley
Ten Kids, No Pets
Slam Book
Just a Summer Romance
Missing Since Monday
With You and Without You
Me and Katie (the Pest)
Stage Fright
Inside Out
Bummer Summer

THE KIDS IN MS. COLMAN'S CLASS series
BABY-SITTERS LITTLE SISTER series
THE BABY-SITTERS CLUB mysteries
THE BABY-SITTERS CLUB series
CALIFORNIA DIARIES series

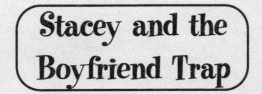

Friends Forever
Baby-sitters Club

Stacey and the Boyfriend Trap

Ann M. Martin

AN
APPLE
PAPERBACK

SCHOLASTIC INC.

New York Toronto London Auckland Sydney

Mexico City New Delhi Hong Kong

The author gratefully acknowledges
Suzanne Weyn
for her help in
preparing this manuscript.

ISBN 0-590-52337-6

12 11 10 9 8 7 6 5 4 3 2 1   0 1 2 3 4 5/0

Printed in the U.S.A.   40

First Scholastic printing, January 2000

❋ Chapter 1

"Oh, please, Dad, pleasepleaseplease," I begged.

He shook his head but twitched his mouth in a way that told me he might give in. "I don't know. Do you really want to go down there, Stacey? It's freezing cold and it's going to be so crowded."

"I can't believe you've lived in New York City all these years and have never gone to Times Square on New Year's Eve! It's less than twenty-five blocks from here," I replied.

"It always seemed like such a hassle," he said. "And when you were little we couldn't drag you out there in the cold."

"People come from all over the world just to be a part of it! Besides, I'm thirteen now, Dad. You don't have to stay home on New Year's Eve because of me anymore. Let's go have some fun!"

Samantha, Dad's girlfriend, took the remote control from the coffee table and turned on the TV. A reporter stood in Times Square, puffing out frosty breath as she spoke. "Although it's only six o'clock, the crowds have already begun to gather here to watch the ball drop at midnight," she said.

"Do you see that?" I said eagerly to Dad.

"I see that she's freezing, and it's going to be a mob scene," he answered.

"It might be fun, Ed," said Samantha.

I smiled at her. Of course, I wish my parents weren't divorced. But, given that they are, I'm lucky that I like the person Dad dates. I was happy he'd found someone who was not only gorgeous but nice.

"I don't want to stand there from now until midnight," he complained.

"We can go after we eat," I said. "Our restaurant isn't far from there."

"True," he agreed. Then he smiled. "Oh, why not? If it's horrible we'll just come home."

"Yess!" I cried.

"Dress warmly," said Dad.

I hurried into my bedroom to change. (After the divorce, Dad found a two-bedroom apartment so he'd have room for me when I visited.)

I began digging through my suitcase for the dress I'd brought to wear.

I was so glad I'd decided to come to New York. At first I hadn't been sure I should come stay with Dad for New Year's Eve. For one thing, I didn't want to leave Mom alone back in Stoneybrook. (Stoneybrook, Connecticut, is where I live most of the time.) But she'd been invited to a party and said she didn't mind if I left.

And then there was my boyfriend, Jeremy Rudolph, to think of. But he didn't mind my going either. His family stays home together on New Year's Eve and watches the ball drop on TV. "You're welcome to come over, but it's pretty boring," he said. Not to mention that I might have felt out of place at his house since we haven't been going out all that long.

Finally, I wasn't even sure if Dad wanted me to visit. What if he'd planned to go out alone with Samantha? When I asked him about that, he told me he and Samantha could go out alone anytime. He definitely wanted to spend New Year's Eve with me.

So there I was. And loving it.

I rummaged through my suitcase. There was my new neon-blue dress, the one I'd bought especially for tonight. But now, thinking about standing outside in the cold, I put it down.

Instead, I picked up my black velvet overalls. They'd be dressy but warm. I also pulled out my thermal long underwear. I'd packed it in case I had the chance to skate in Central Park over the weekend. I was glad I had it now.

I put on the thermals, then a long-sleeved white shirt, and, finally, the overalls. I slid on a black headband decorated with white peace signs and pulled wisps of my blonde hair out around my face.

Then I took out my makeup bag. Dad doesn't like me to wear much makeup. But if I didn't glob it on, he probably wouldn't even notice. (My mom would notice in an instant, but she allows it.)

So I brushed on some mascara. (Just enough.) And I added some tinted lip gloss. Then I pulled on my ankle-high black boots and was done.

"Great outfit," Samantha said when I came out.

"Thanks," I replied.

Dad had been dragging things out of the front hall closet. We couldn't see him because the open door blocked our view. But when he stepped into the living room, Samantha and I burst out laughing.

He was bundled up as if he were planning to

spend New Year's Eve in Antarctica. Ski mask. Scarf. Heavy gloves. Down parka.

"It's not *that* cold, Ed," Samantha said with a snort.

He lifted his ski mask. "You wait," he said. "Wait until you're standing out there on Broadway. It's like a wind tunnel."

"You'll definitely be prepared, Dad," I said, pulling my jacket from the closet.

Samantha shrugged into her fake-fur coat and pulled on her gloves. Then we left the apartment.

The moment we walked out onto 65th Street, something cold hit my nose. "Snow!" I cried, lifting my gloved hand to catch another flake.

"Great," said Dad grumpily. "We'll be in Times Square in a blizzard."

"It's a flurry, Ed." Samantha laughed.

Dad waved down a cab and we traveled to a restaurant called Un, Deux, Trois, which is French for one, two, three. (The restaurant's street address is 123.) It's one of Dad's and my favorites.

The holiday lights were glowing. No place is more beautiful at this time of year than New York City. At least that's my opinion. Of course, I'm a city fan, so I think most everything about Manhattan is awesome.

The restaurant was crowded with people waiting to be seated, but everyone seemed cheerful. Our table was ready right away. We made our way toward the back, and I gazed up at the ceiling, which is painted with clouds.

I looked around at the other diners. They all seemed so glamorous. (Not like in Stoneybrook, where the people are more . . . well . . . regular.)

Dad and Samantha ordered escargots to start. Even though it may be very sophisticated, eating snails grosses me out. (That's what escargots are, snails.) I had shrimp cocktail.

We all ate lobster for our main course.

Everything was wonderful, except that my thermals began to itch a bit and make me feel too warm.

Dad and Samantha held hands across the table. They seemed very much in love. It made me think about Jeremy. He's adorable. I wondered what he was doing at that moment.

Then, to my surprise, I thought of Ethan too.

Ethan Carroll is my former boyfriend. I broke up with him just days before I began seeing Jeremy. We had said we would stay friends, but so far it wasn't working out that way. We weren't fighting or anything like that. We just didn't call each other much.

Ethan lives here in the city. So if I didn't make the effort, it was easy to avoid seeing him.

Tonight, though, as I ate, I imagined running into him in Times Square. He'd be with friends, but he'd leave them to be with me. Maybe we'd even kiss at midnight — just as friends.

Even though I was with Dad and Samantha, I guess I was feeling a little lonely. I'd recently had a huge blowup with my very closest friend, Claudia Kishi. We hadn't spoken, except for a few coldly polite words, in weeks.

It had been over Jeremy. She liked him first. But he didn't like her — not in that boyfriend-girlfriend way. He told me he wouldn't have asked her out whether he'd met me or not. Still, she blamed me for stealing him from her. Which is totally unfair of her. He was never hers to begin with.

Even though it made me furious every time I thought about how childish she was acting, I still missed her. A best friend is a big thing to lose. I have other good friends — great friends — but Claudia was my best bud. Since I'm an only child, I think we were as close as sisters. At least sometimes.

"Dessert?" Dad said as the waiter cleared away our plates.

I scowled at him. He knows I can't eat French pastries. That's because I have a condition called diabetes. My body doesn't regulate the amount of sugar in my blood the way it should. To stay healthy, I have to give myself injections of insulin daily and follow a carefully balanced diet. Most sweets are out.

"Don't look at me like that," Dad defended himself. "There's fruit on the menu."

"Oh," I said, brightening. Fruit was okay. "Great."

So, while Dad and Samantha shared a slice of cheesecake, I munched on a dish of raspberries, strawberries, and slivered almonds.

After we paid the bill, the three of us bundled up again and headed several blocks over to Times Square.

Dad had been right about the wind. The minute we turned the corner onto Broadway an icy blast roared up the back of my jacket. I didn't care, though. I was too excited.

The area was completely packed with people. Some were speaking languages I couldn't even identify. It seemed as if people from every country on earth were there.

Dad — the one who hadn't even wanted to come — was the most swept up in the party spirit. He began wishing strangers a happy New Year and joking with them. He bought us hats and blowers from a street vendor. I loved seeing him so happy.

We made our way as close to the center of things as we could. There was still another hour until the ball dropped. I talked to people around me and blew my horn. The time went quickly. It was about ten to twelve when someone's hand touched my shoulder from behind.

My heart jumped. Ethan?

I turned around.

No. It was a reporter from Channel 4 News. "Young lady, what brings you out here this cold New Year's Eve?" she asked as the wind tossed her hair.

A man with a large TV camera stood behind her and the camera was on me!

I smiled directly into it. Around me, people tried to squeeze into the shot, waving at the camera. "Tonight this is the center of the world!" I answered, almost shouting to be heard. "It's the best, most fun place to be!"

"All right," the reporter said, laughter in her voice. "Thank you."

She moved on to interview another person. "I hope someone sees that on TV," Dad said when I turned back to Samantha and him.

"Me too," I exclaimed. I wondered which of my friends might see it. Or Mom? I hoped so.

Only five more minutes to go. I suddenly realized I hadn't made any New Year's resolutions. My mind raced. What did I want to do better in the coming year?

I hate to admit this, but the first thing that jumped into my mind was to pick better colors in clothing. I'd recently read a magazine article about what colors a person should wear to go with her skin and hair type. Apparently I've been making all the wrong choices, just grabbing colors I like instead of thinking about how they look on me.

Oh, you're not that shallow, I scolded myself. I tried to come up with something more serious.

My grades are good. I'm not too sloppy. I don't need to lose weight. What should I resolve to do?

Then two faces popped into my mind. Claudia's and Ethan's. "I resolve to be a better friend," I whispered. (Even though no one in that noisy crowd would have noticed if I'd shouted.)

I wanted to end this fight with Claudia. It was stupid and I had to make her see that. Both of us were too stubborn and proud to break the silence. But I was going to try to forget my pride and talk to her.

That idea made me feel light inside. And the happiness told me it was the right thing to do.

As for Ethan, well, it didn't look as though I would run into him tonight after all. But my fantasy made me realize how much I missed him. He probably felt strange about calling me, not sure if I really wanted him to. And up until tonight, I hadn't been certain I *could* be friends with him. Now it seemed possible. I'd call him as soon as I had the chance.

Loud voices shook me out of my thoughts. The crowd was shouting numbers. The shiny New Year's ball was starting to descend. The countdown to midnight had begun!

I joined in. "Six! Five! Four!" Dad took one hand and Samantha took the other. "Three! Two! One! Happy New Year!"

We hugged and kissed. All around us, horns blew and people cheered. I looked up at the glittering ball, feeling excited about what the coming year would bring.

❋ Chapter 2

The next morning I didn't open my eyes until the bright midday light hit my face. Voices were coming from the living room. Propping myself up on my elbows, I listened.

Beep. "Hello, Ed. Just calling to wish you a happy New Year."

Beep. "Happy New Year, Eddie, you son of a gun!"

Dad was listening to his answering machine.

I snuggled back under my covers. Then a familiar voice made me pop up again.

Beep. "Stacey, Stacey! I saw you on TV! Way to go!"

It was Kristy Thomas, one of my friends from home.

Springing out of bed, I hurried into the living

room. "Kristy saw me, Dad!" I cried excitedly. "I really was on TV! Oh, I wish *I'd* seen it!"

Dad, still in his robe, sat in the big armchair beside the answering machine. He smiled and nodded as the machine continued playing his messages.

Beep. "Stacey! Hi! It's Mom. Happy New Year! I was so amazed to see you on TV. I was at my party and suddenly there you were. How exciting!"

Then her tone grew serious. "I assume your father was with you. Oh, and happy New Year, Ed. You *were* with Stacey, weren't you? I didn't see you."

She lightened up again. "Well, anyway, you can tell me all about it on Sunday. I'll be at the station to pick you up, as we planned. 'Bye."

Dad rolled his eyes and shook his head. "As if I would really let you go to Times Square on New Year's Eve by yourself."

That made me laugh. "She just worries," I said. My parents are civil enough, but their relationship isn't exactly what you'd call warm and wonderful.

Beep. "Hi, Stacey. It's me, Mary Anne." Mary Anne Spier is another of my good friends at home. "My dad saw you on TV. He caught you on tape! I was so surprised. Happy New Year!"

"All right!" I cried. "I'll be able to see it."

"Great!" said Dad. "I hoped someone would

catch it. If you get the tape for me I'll have it copied."

Beep. "Hi, guys, it's Samantha. Call me when you wake up and get this message. How about brunch at my place? 'Bye."

Dad looked at me. "How about it? She makes a great western omelet."

"Can I let you know in a minute?" I replied. "I just want to make one call."

"Okay. Decide by the time I'm out of the shower."

"Thanks." I had just remembered my resolution. There was no sense wasting time.

I called Ethan. "Stacey!" he answered, recognizing my voice. "What's been happening?"

He didn't sound at all annoyed that I hadn't called him earlier.

"Would you like to go have coffee?" I asked.

He laughed. "You mean the kind of *go have coffee* when we never drink coffee?" he asked.

"Yup." It was a little joke between us. We're not old enough to drink coffee, but when we first met, we tried to act cool and we'd say, "Let's go for coffee." Ethan is fifteen, two years older than me. (He's in high school. I'm in the eighth grade.) So it took me awhile just to act like myself and stop trying to impress him with my *maturity*.

"I'll be right over," Ethan said.

"Excellent!"

Dad emerged from the bathroom, toweling his hair. "Did you make your call?" he asked.

"Yes. And if you don't mind, I'd like to go have breakfast with Ethan this morning."

"Oh? I thought you two split up."

"We're friends," I told him. Dad made a skeptical face. "Don't you think it's possible?" I asked.

"No," he replied bluntly.

"Well, you're wrong." Was I sure about that? No. "At least I hope you are," I added more cautiously.

"You can go," he said. "Remember, though, you have a train to catch."

"Okay."

Dad left while I was in my room getting ready. I suppose if a boy is just a friend, a girl shouldn't spend a lot of time getting ready to see him.

I couldn't help it, though.

I wanted to look good for Ethan. So I wore my best jeans and a soft blue sweater I'd just received for Christmas. I went a little heavier with the makeup since Dad was already gone. Then I brushed my hair until it shone.

When I was ready, it occurred to me to call Jeremy. But I didn't feel like it. My mind was set on seeing Ethan. Mixing up boys like that was confusing.

The lobby buzzer sounded and I hit the button. "Ethan?" I asked.

"Yup," he answered and I hit another button to let him in. When he rang our bell, I made the necessary New York check through the peephole. (No New Yorker opens a door without first seeing who's on the other side of it.)

Then I yanked the door open wide. "Ethan!" I cried.

"Hi," he said.

"You cut your hair."

He nodded and made an uncertain face. "It's pretty short, isn't it?"

Ethan used to have beautiful long dark hair. This was practically a buzz cut. It made his eyes look huge. And the one earring he wore was definitely on view.

"I like it," I pronounced after a moment's study.

He stepped inside while I pulled on my jacket, hat, and gloves. Then I locked the door behind me and we walked to the elevator.

"So? What's been happening?" I asked as we rode down together.

"I'm really liking my new art teacher," he began. Ethan is an art student and a talented painter. "This guy is a real working artist." We entered the lobby and walked out of the building. The snow had piled up. In some cases we had to walk into the street, around unshoveled patches of sidewalk. "His name is Van Sant. He's doing cool, experimental work," Ethan continued, extending his hand to help me over a mound of snow.

"I'd like to see it."

"You might be able to," Ethan said excitedly. "I was going to call you about this."

I made a disbelieving face at him. He hadn't called me about anything in awhile.

"No kidding," he insisted. "I was going to call you because this guy's having an exhibition at the Stoneybrook Museum."

"Wow!" I cried. "I can't imagine the boring old Stoneybrook Museum featuring an experimental artist. How did he land there?"

Ethan shrugged. "Maybe he knows people at the museum. I'm not sure. Anyway, he's invited all of his students to the opening of his show."

"Awesome," I said. I know Ethan loves openings. He and I had gone to some at the art gallery where he works part-time. Going to them always made me feel very grown-up and sophisticated.

"I'm not sure I'll make it, though," Ethan went on. "It's in two weeks, on a Saturday. But if I do, do you want to go with me? As friends, I mean."

"That would be great. Give me a call if you decide to go."

We had arrived at our favorite coffee shop.

Closed!

"It's New Year's Day," I reminded him. "I bet a lot of places will be closed."

"You're right. How about the big bookstore café? It might be open. But it's a long way from here."

I didn't mind the walk, so we turned and headed uptown. The blocks flew as we talked about this and that. He asked about Claudia. I'd brought her to the city with me a few times and she'd met Ethan.

"Don't ask," I said. "We had the biggest, stupidest fight."

"What about?"

Should I tell him it was about a guy? Would that make him feel weird? It might. But if we were really going to have a friendship, I had to be honest. "We both liked the same guy," I told him.

Ethan nodded. "Don't tell me. *You're* the one *he* liked."

"How did you know?"

"I know what's to like about you," he said. His voice was pretty even, but I thought I heard a hint of sadness in it.

It made me want to change the subject. Fast. "Are you still taking that Sunday course at the Artist's Studio?" I asked.

Our breakup began partly because of that art course. Ethan and I had so little time together, and I was angry that he signed up for a class that met at a time when I could actually see him.

Now it didn't matter anymore.

"It's an awesome class," he began. By the time he finished telling me about it, we were at the bookstore, which, luckily was open.

The café was snuggled in the very back of the store. It was empty except for the employees. It was like having this huge, amazing, book-filled space to ourselves.

We sat and had tea and croissants. Then we wandered the endless stacks of books, browsing and talking about the different subjects.

I might never have left, but I happened to look up at the clock on the wall. "My train!" I cried in alarm. "I've got to go!"

"Bummer," said Ethan.

"I know." I was hopping around anxiously. "You stay and browse. I have to run."

"I'll come with you," he offered.

"No, you don't have to." I began to back down the aisle of books. "Call me about the Stoneybrook art show!"

I kept thinking of Ethan as I hailed a cab back to Dad's apartment. Dad was home when I arrived. "Better move," he told me.

Without taking off my jacket, I ran into my room. I threw my things in the suitcase and packed in record time.

Thanks to all the rushing around, I was on time. I dozed all the way to Stoneybrook on the nearly empty train. If the conductor hadn't woken me up at the stop, I don't know where I'd have wound up.

Mom sat in her idling car, waiting. "Happy New

Year, star," she greeted me when I climbed in. "You looked great on TV."

"Thanks," I said. "Mary Anne has it on tape."

She told me all about her party as we drove home. I gazed out the window as I listened. It looked a lot snowier up here in Stoneybrook than it had in the city. I love the city, but I'm always happy to come home to Stoneybrook.

"There's mail in the backseat," Mom told me. "It's from yesterday. I forgot to take it out of the car. There's a letter for you."

I wondered if Claudia had written me a peace-making letter. I hoped so.

I reached back and grabbed the stack of mail. There was no return address on my letter. And I didn't recognize the handwriting.

"Who is it from?" Mom asked, turning the corner onto our street.

"I don't know." I began ripping open the envelope. Before I even read it, I turned it over and found the signature.

I couldn't believe it. "This must be some kind of a joke," I said.

"Who is it from?" Mom asked again.

"Toby."

"Who?"

"Maybe I never told you about him," I said. "He was this guy I met in Sea City."

"Is he someone you like?"

I thought for a moment. "He used to be," I told her.

❀ Chapter 3

I flashed back to that summer at the New Jersey shore. In many ways it was a great one. Mary Anne and I met these two guys, Alex and Toby. Cousins, and both really cute.

Toby was the one I liked. I thought he was adorable. He seemed to like me too. Finally, after lots of flirting and hanging out, the big moment arrived. He kissed me.

It was my first kiss, and let me tell you — it was a great one.

I thought we were at the beginning of an amazing romance. But Toby thought it was the end. I'm not kidding. The next time we saw each other he dumped me.

This was his reason: I was getting too serious. He needed to be free to see other girls.

What a jerk!

I saw him the summer after that . . . and he chased my friend Mallory around. Fortunately for her, she realized what a flirt he was before he hurt her feelings. And he didn't pay much attention to me. Which was fine. But why would he be writing to me now?

Inside the house, I shrugged off my jacket and sat down to read the letter.

Hey, Stacey.

Surprise! Bet you never expected to hear from me. Here I am, though. Guess what! You may be seeing me in person very soon. If you want to, that is.

Hmm. He lived nowhere near Stoneybrook. As I recalled, his home was somewhere in New Jersey.

My big brother is taking a tour of Eastern colleges. Yours truly will be forced along for this jolly family road trip. What could make this nightmare bearable? The fact that we'll be zooming down I-95 past a town called Stoneybrook, Connecticut.

The moment I spotted your town on the map, I said to myself, I wonder how Stacey McGill is doing? Wouldn't it be great to see her again!

I know we didn't end our relationship on the best note. That's because I acted like a moron. A big jerk. Sorry. I don't know what was the matter with me then.

I put the letter down. I was impressed that he could admit that he'd acted like a jerk. If a person knows he's been a jerk, does that make him less of a jerk?

I hope you believe that a person can change. I sure have. In lots of ways. How about it? Would you like a visit from your old beach buddy? I could jump out of the car on I-95 and run the rest of the way to your house. Seriously, I think I can convince Dad to make a little side trip.

Can you e-mail me? If you can, my address is Tobythegreat.

I tapped the letter absentmindedly, wondering what I should do. Did I really want Toby to visit? I wasn't sure.

Had Mary Anne received anything from Alex, Toby's cousin? Maybe this was some big joke the two of them had cooked up together.

I went to the kitchen phone and called her. "Hi, it's me, Stacey," I said when Mary Anne picked up.

"You looked great on TV!" she cried. "I couldn't believe it. Dad's out now trying to find some place to have the tape copied. Meanwhile, Sharon decided to throw together a small New Year's open house. So come on over. Invite your mom. Bring Jeremy if you want."

"Do you think that's a good idea?" I asked.

"Claudia's in New Jersey with her family, visiting relatives," she informed me.

"All right, I'll call him. Listen, did you get any mail from Alex? You know, from Sea City?"

"Alex? No. Why?"

I told her about the letter from Toby.

"That's weird," she said. "I wonder what he's up to."

"You think he's up to something?"

"I don't know. What are you going to tell him?"

"I have no idea. "

I decided not to tell him anything right away.

Instead I called Jeremy.

One thing I really hate about the winter is that it gets dark so early. By the time Jeremy arrived at my house, it looked like night already, even though it was only six o'clock.

"Happy New Year," he greeted me as he stepped inside.

"Same to you," I replied, laying a light kiss on his lips.

I smiled up at him, happy to see him. Jeremy has this friendly, puppy-dog look about him that just knocks me out.

I grabbed my jacket and called up the stairs to Mom. She was going to follow us in a few minutes.

The moment Jeremy and I stepped outside, I shoved my gloved hands into my pockets. "Wow! It's cold!"

Jeremy nodded, frosty breath streaming from his mouth. He hooked his arm through mine and we hurried down the walkway.

"What did you do today?" he asked.

Should I tell him about Ethan? He'd been pretty bent out of shape when he'd first learned about Ethan. (Claudia had told Jeremy he was just a rebound boyfriend until I reunited with Ethan. Thank you very much, Claudia!)

Considering his reaction then, I decided it might be better not to tell him now. "Just hung around," I said. I hoped if I was vague enough it wouldn't be a real lie. "How about you? What did you do?"

"I went to the mall with Erica Blumberg and Claudia."

"Claudia!" I gasped. "I thought she was in New Jersey."

"She left at about two o'clock."

"How did you wind up with them?" I'm not the jealous type, honest! But I wasn't crazy about the idea of Jeremy hanging around with Claudia, who was probably still madly in love with him.

"Erica called me and then she asked if it was all right if Claudia came too. I didn't mind."

I just stared at him.

"Do you mind about Erica?" he asked.

"Erica? No! What about Claudia?"

"You know I only like Claudia as a friend," he insisted. "I've told you that so many times. Are you jealous?"

"No," I said, more sharply than I'd meant to. "And I don't want to tell you what to do or who to hang out with. But I don't want to lose you."

He grinned. "You're not losing me. It's not like I was alone with either one of them. It was a pal thing."

"You're right. I was silly to worry," I said.

If only I could believe what I was saying . . .

✿ Chapter 4

Believe it or not, I was happy to go back to school after the vacation. When the vacation had started I'd thought, *Great! No homework! Sleeping late!* By the end of it, though, I was bored. It's so easy to see your friends when you're at school. You don't have to make plans or anything. They're all right there.

Besides that, I missed school itself — especially my favorite subject, math.

Most kids can't believe math is my best subject. I guess that's because so many students struggle with it. It's always come easily to me, though. And I enjoy it. Also, I have the best math teacher in the world, Mr. Zizmore. He's wonderful. He's super-enthusiastic about math. (He once told us that for fun he and his wife — also a mathematician — sit around and try to solve difficult math problems.) He spreads that excitement to his students.

So there I was, smiling, thrilled to be back in his class again.

Then he dropped the bomb.

"I have something to tell you," he began. The serious expression on his face made us all quiet down fast. We looked at him with total attention.

"These next two weeks will be my last here at Stoneybrook Middle School."

Silence.

Everyone was stunned. What was he saying? Could it be true?

Then the class exploded with the sound of kids asking questions all at once.

"Why?"

"Where are you going?"

"Are you sick?"

He gestured to quiet us down. Slowly, everyone stopped talking. "My wife has received a wonderful job offer to work for NASA in Houston, Texas."

"Houston, we have a problem," Pete Black joked from the back. We laughed. A little.

Mr. Zizmore smiled. "It *was* a problem for us," he admitted. "We really didn't want to leave. But we spent the vacation in endless discussion and decided that the job is too great an opportunity for her to pass up."

I just sat there with my jaw hanging open. This couldn't be happening. My favorite teacher on earth couldn't be leaving. He just couldn't be!

"What will *you* do?" asked a girl in the front row.

"I'll still teach math. I've already secured a position at a high school in Houston."

Lucky kids in Houston, I thought grumpily. *How dare they steal my best teacher!* I raised my hand. "Couldn't your wife fly back and forth or something? You belong here."

"I felt that way at first too," Mr. Zizmore replied, shaking his head. "But you can't be afraid of change."

I rolled my eyes.

"I'll miss all of you," he added.

I only half listened for the rest of the class. I couldn't imagine Mr. Z. not being here. It didn't matter who replaced him. There'd never be another Mr. Zizmore.

When class was finished, everyone shuffled out. I didn't want to leave, but I couldn't think of a reason to stay.

As I passed his desk, Mr. Z. called to me.

I turned.

"I saw you on TV on New Year's Eve."

"You did?"

"You looked as if you were having fun."

"I was," I said. "Do you really have to go?"

He smiled sadly. "I do. This is the chance of a lifetime for Angela."

I sighed. "It won't be the same without you."

"Thanks, Stacey. But you, of all my students, will do fine without me. You have the talent to be an outstanding mathematician. I hope you decide to use that gift."

"Thanks," I said.

He stood up. "We still have two weeks together. I'm sure they'll be challenging."

I shot him a quick smile and left.

"Bummer, isn't it?" said Pete, who was hanging around in the hall when I shut the classroom door behind me.

"Totally," I agreed.

Pete and I were sort of involved awhile back. Not seriously. But we went out a few times. Since then we'd become friendly. I worked on a film project in the same group with him. The project relaxed things between us and we're real, honest-to-goodness friends now. I'd even tried to fix him up with Mary

Anne after she broke up with Logan Bruno, her old boyfriend, but it didn't work out.

Like me, Pete is good at math. And Mr. Z. is also one of his favorite teachers.

"I waited for you because I have an idea, and I want to hear what you think of it," he said. "How about giving Mr. Z. some kind of party before he leaves?"

"That's a great idea!"

"How do we get started? Should we ask permission or something?"

"I suppose we could talk to Mr. Kingbridge."

"Mr. Kingbridge?" Pete cried. The horror on his face made it seem as if I'd suggested we see Dracula.

"Oh, come on," I said with a laugh. "He's a good guy."

"If you say so."

"I don't see how we can avoid it. We can't throw a party at school without permission, can we?"

"I guess not. A little class thing, maybe. But not a real party. Okay. You talk to him as soon as you can."

"Me?" I shrieked. "Alone? I don't think so. You're coming with me."

Pete sighed. "All right. Tomorrow. I need tonight to work up the nerve."

"There's nothing to be scared of."

"Then why didn't you want to do it alone?"

"Ummmm . . ." Maybe it *was* a little scary. Mr. Kingbridge was the assistant principal, after all. He wasn't the friendliest guy — more of an authority figure than a pal.

"Got you there," Pete teased.

"No, you didn't. I want you to come with me because we're in this project together. Right?"

"Okay, partner. Meet you at your locker tomorrow during study period."

"See you then," I agreed as he headed off down the hall. I hoped our idea would work.

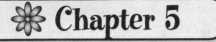 **Chapter 5**

The moment Pete and I entered Mr. Kingbridge's office on Tuesday, during study period, I knew how silly we'd been to worry about talking to him.

He sat behind his big desk and smiled at us when we walked in. "What's up?" he said. "Talk to me."

He motioned for us to sit on the two chairs in front of his desk.

"It's Mr. Zizmore," I began as I sat down.

"We'd like to give him a going-away party," Pete continued. "We figured we should talk to you about it."

Mr. Kingbridge clapped his hands together. "An excellent idea! The math department was planning a small good-bye party, but student participation will really make him happy."

"Then we can do it?" Pete asked, leaning forward eagerly in his chair.

"Absolutely. You can join the faculty party. How would a week from Saturday be?"

"Fine," I answered. "Are you sure Mr. Zizmore will still be around?"

He nodded. "Yes. He's not leaving until the following Wednesday."

"It's perfect, then," I said. "Having it on Saturday will surprise him too. He'll leave SMS on Friday thinking he's seen us all for the last time. But how will we get him back to school on Saturday?"

"Hmmm." Mr. Kingbridge considered this. Then he brightened. "I know. I'll say my wife and I want to take him and his wife out to dinner to say farewell. I'll let his wife in on the secret. Then I'll pretend I need to stop by the school for something."

"Terrific!" I cried.

"Put a committee together," Mr. Kingbridge suggested. "You students can take over the decorations, and invitations too. I can get you some money from our faculty fund."

"That's great," I said as I stood up. "We'll organize some kids to work on this and let you know what's happening."

"All right. Keep in touch with me and let me know how you're doing."

"We will. Thanks," Pete said as we left his office.

Neither of us spoke until we were in the hall. "That went very well," I commented.

"Mr. Kingbridge is a good guy," Pete replied.

Glancing at the hall clock, I saw we had about twenty minutes of study period left. "Let's go to the library and plan what we have to do," I suggested.

"Okay."

In the library we found seats together.

"The first thing we need to do is figure out who to invite."

"Anyone who had Mr. Z. as a teacher," Pete replied. "We could even invite some of his old students who are in high school. Or even older people."

I nodded and wrote "Invitations" on the list.

"Maybe a kid with older brothers and sisters could handle this," I said. "Claudia's sister, Janine, had Mr. Z. I think. She might . . ." My voice trailed off.

Contacting Janine would mean talking to Claudia.

I remembered my New Year's resolution.

This might give me the excuse I needed to call Claudia. Then I could take it from there.

"What?" Pete asked. I must have zoned out on him for a minute.

"Oh, nothing," I replied. "Claudia and I have been mad at each other lately. I was wondering whether I should ask her to work with us. That's all."

Pete looked shocked. "You guys have always been so tight. I can't believe it."

"I can't either, really," I admitted.

"I hope you make up," Pete said. "What are you guys fighting about?"

"It's so stupid — believe me — you don't want to know."

"If you say so. This is going to be fun," Pete commented as the buzzer signaled the end of the period. We gathered our books and stood up to leave.

We left the classroom together. "I'm so excited about this," I said. "Mr. Z. will be totally — "

I was going to say "blown away."

Instead, I was blown away.

In the hall, right in front of me, stood Wes Ellenberg!

"Hi, Stacey," he said, shooting me his gorgeous smile.

He remembered my name! I stood there, stunned.

He nodded toward Pete. "Hi."

I should explain. Wes did his student teaching here at SMS, with Mr. Z. as his supervisor. Then he substituted for Mr. Z. for a few weeks.

He's extremely cute, and he looks younger than he is. I had the most gigantic crush on him! I'd spent way too much class time calculating how old he'd be when I was twenty. (No more than twenty-nine, I guessed.) And when I was twenty-five he'd only be about thirty-four. Twenty-five and thirty-four were totally acceptable ages for two people to date. (And marry.)

Only now — at thirteen and twenty-two — did the age difference seem outrageous.

Despite our ages, I'd had the feeling that Wes had liked me as a person. We even danced together once at a school dance.

I had decided the trick was to find a way to contact him again when I was older.

I was clueless as to how I would do that. But it might happen. You never know.

"What are you doing here?" I asked, forcing myself back to the present.

"I've been certified as a teacher for awhile, but I haven't found a full-time job," he explained.

"Bummer," I commented.

He nodded. "Tell me about it. There's some

hope, though. Mr. Zizmore called to tell me he was leaving, so I came down to apply for his job. I was on my way to his classroom to talk to him for a minute."

My head reeled. Wes might be my teacher! He was as cute as ever. If he landed the job it would be wonderful.

But terrible!

How would I ever pay attention to the math work, with Wes in front of me each day? How would I keep from daydreaming about the two of us together?

Wes shifted from foot to foot. I realized he wanted to leave.

"Well, good luck," I said. "I hope you get the job."

"Thanks. Me too," he replied.

"Listen," I told him. "There's a going-away party for Mr. Z. a week from Saturday, here at school. It's a surprise. Would you like to come?"

"Sure. What time?"

"I don't know yet. We'll send you an invitation." I pulled out a blank sheet of paper from my notebook. "What's your address?"

"Can you e-mail me?"

"Sure," I said, handing him the paper and a pen. "Write down your e-mail address."

He wrote it down and handed the paper back to me with a smile.

"I'd better run before Mr. Z. starts his next class," Wes said. " 'Bye!"

" 'Bye!" I said, watching him go. I glanced down at his e-mail name.

Mathguy.

How cool.

"Do you really want him to get the job?" Pete asked.

I'd nearly forgotten he was there. "Yes! Don't you?"

Pete shrugged. "I didn't think he was such a hot teacher."

I stared at him blankly. Was Wes a good teacher? I wasn't sure. As far as I was concerned, he was just generally great.

"He was boring," Pete added.

"Boring?" Wes boring?

Never.

❀ Chapter 6

The next day as I headed to my locker I had that time-warp feeling again. There stood my old boyfriend Robert Brewster, obviously waiting for me.

But why?

Robert and I had dated steadily for a pretty long time. I mean, it was a serious thing. But it had been over for awhile.

"Hi," I said as I neared my locker.

"Hi, Stace."

He was still adorable, with his deep, dark eyes and wavy brown hair. We hadn't talked much lately. The last time we'd been together was at a dance. We went just as friends. It had been a good night. We felt very close. But not as boyfriend and girlfriend.

"What's happening?" I asked him.

"I wanted to talk to you about the Mr. Z. party. Pete told me about it."

Pete and Robert have become friends lately. I was happy about that. Robert has been pretty down in the dumps. Really depressed. He and I spent a lot of time talking about it. He wasn't exactly sure what was wrong. But he knew one thing. His old friends didn't appeal to him any longer. He needed to make some new ones. These days, he seemed better, not so unhappy. And he'd become friendly with Pete.

Still, his old megawatt smile hadn't returned. I was always a little worried about him.

"Are you going to sign up to work on it?" I asked. "You had Mr. Z. last year, after all."

"You wouldn't mind?"

I shot him a puzzled look. "Why should I mind?"

He shrugged. "I want to give you your space."

"Thanks for thinking of it," I said. "But we don't have to worry about that stuff anymore. I think we're solid friends now. At least, that's how I feel. Don't you?"

"Yeah," he agreed a little shyly. "I only wanted to check."

I smiled at him. "How have you been lately?" I asked gently.

43

"All right. I guess. I feel a lot better about stuff, most of the time."

"That's good. It would be great to have you on the committee. We'll be handing around a sign-up sheet at lunch. We're doing it then so Mr. Z. doesn't see."

"Cool," Robert said. "I'll sign up for sure. See ya."

"Later," I replied as Robert walked off. I thought how sweet he could be. I hoped working on the party would be fun for him.

As I stood there, a weird thought hit me. I'd be spending a lot of time with Pete and Robert, two guys I'd once dated, over the next week or so. Would this bother Jeremy?

And at that moment he rounded a corner and headed toward me. "Jeremy!" I greeted him. "Have you heard the news?"

"I don't know. What news?" he asked, leaning against the locker next to mine.

I told him about the party.

"No, I didn't hear. That's nice of you to do," he said.

"Do you want to sign up?"

"Me? He's never been my teacher."

"It doesn't matter. I want you to work on the

party with me. We don't have any classes or clubs together. This would be fun."

"But I'd feel strange. I don't know the other kids from his classes."

"This is a good way to get to know them. You can't just hang out with Erica and Claudia all the time."

As soon as I mentioned Erica and Claudia, I knew I sounded as if I were jealous or something. But it was too late to take it back.

"I had a feeling it bothered you that I went to the mall with them," he said.

"No! It didn't!" I insisted. "Not at all. Come on. I already told you I didn't mind."

He looked at me skeptically.

"Wouldn't you like to make more friends, though?" I went on. "You just moved here. You don't know many people. And I'll be busy with this for awhile. If you work on it with me, at least we'll be together."

"Will you be working on it that much?" he asked.

"Pete and I will be pretty much in charge of the decorations committee," I said.

"Who's Pete?" There was an uneasy sound in his voice.

"Pete Black. He's in my class. Working on the party was really his idea to begin with."

"Then how did you get involved?"

"Pete knows how much I like Mr. Z., so he spoke to me about it. That's all." That was the truth. I didn't have to mention that I had once dated Pete. Or that we were even friends.

"Does this Pete guy like you?" Jeremy asked.

"No-o," I answered, rolling my eyes.

"All right. I'll sign up."

"Don't do it just to keep an eye on me."

"I'm *not*. I want us to spend time together. And it wouldn't hurt to meet some new kids."

I smiled at him and squeezed his hand. "Great! I typed up the list last night. You can sign up right now."

I pulled the list from my locker. "Here." I handed it to him. "Sign up, then bring the list to the lunchroom. That's where we're going to pass it around."

Later, as the list went around the lunchroom, I sat at my usual table with my friends, watching kids sign up. "Look how many kids are volunteering. We'll have plenty of help," I commented.

"I never had Mr. Zizmore, but I'll sign up," my friend Kristy offered.

"Excellent," I said. Kristy is a real take-charge person with a zillion ideas and tons of energy. She would be a huge help.

"I'll work on the party," said our friend Abby Stevenson.

"Cool." I said. Abby's a lot of fun.

"I'd like to help too," Mary Anne volunteered.

This seemed like the perfect time to talk to Claudia. Lately, though we continued to sit together at lunch, each of us had been acting as if the other one weren't there.

I decided to forget that.

"Claudia, you'd be great on this decoration committee," I said. That was true. Claudia is so artistic and creative. "And we also need help from someone who can contact some of Mr. Z.'s older students. I was thinking that since Janine had Mr. Zizmore and she's in high school now, you could ask her for the names and addresses of some of the kids who . . ."

My voice faded as I realized Claudia was deliberately ignoring me. She'd turned her head and was gazing around the lunchroom as if I weren't speaking to her at all. She ran one hand absentmindedly through her hair.

"*Excuse me,*" I said pointedly. "Claudia, are you there?"

Slowly, she turned back to me. "Did you say something?"

I glared at her. I knew perfectly well she'd heard every word I'd said.

"Never mind," I snapped at her. "I didn't say anything."

"Good."

So much for resolutions.

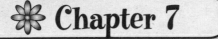

Chapter 7

On Saturday morning, I woke up feeling panicked. I knew there were a zillion things I needed to do. And I couldn't remember what they were!

"Okay, think, Stacey," I told myself as I sat up in bed, the early morning sun streaming through the window. "The party. What do I have to do for that?"

No idea came to me. The sign-up sheet wouldn't even be completed until Monday.

"Homework?" I asked myself out loud.

I just had to read a chapter in history.

What about friends? Had I said I'd do anything with anyone? I thought hard. No.

The panic lifted. I'd been so busy all week that I'd fallen into the habit of rushing around. But today was free.

That felt great!

I could do whatever I wanted.

I swung my feet over the side of the bed, stood up, and headed for my closet. Then I stopped.

What did I want to do?

I decided it would be a good time to catch up with my friends. A perfect time, actually. Jeremy's cousins were coming over and they were going sledding. I didn't have to worry about neglecting him.

Claudia was visiting family friends in Stamford (which is the nearest city to Stoneybrook). With her out of the way for the day, I could hang with my other friends without her angry eyes burning into me.

I pulled on khakis and a sweater, then ran downstairs and phoned Mary Anne. "Hi, it's Stacey. What are you doing today?"

"Thinking," Mary Anne answered.

"About what?"

"My room."

"Okay," I said with a laugh. "Why are you thinking about your room?"

She laughed in return. "My new room, I mean. The one I'll have when they finish our new house."

Several months ago, Mary Anne's old house was burned to the ground in a fire. Luckily, no one was hurt. She and her parents relocated to a rented house next door to Claudia's.

It's only temporary. They've already cleared the burned debris from the place where their house used to be, and are turning their old barn into a house.

"The architect and designer asked me to tell them what I want my new room to look like," she went on. "I have to tell them by Monday."

"Cool. What are you thinking?"

"I'm not sure. Sharon suggested we go to the home stores in the mall for some ideas." (Sharon is Mary Anne's stepmom. Her birth mother died when Mary Anne was a baby.)

"That sounds like fun," I said.

"Do you want to come with us?"

"Definitely."

"Great. Kristy's coming too. We'll stop by for you in about an hour."

We had a blast at Washington Mall that afternoon. First we stole some time to look at clothes. Then CDs. Finally we got down to business. We went to Bookcenter, a bookstore, to do some research on Mary Anne's new room. Bookcenter lets you sit at tables and look at the books before you buy them.

Kristy, Mary Anne, and I each grabbed an interior design book and brought it to a table. Each book showed pages and pages of different rooms and how you could put them together. We turned to the bedroom chapters.

Sharon was nearby, browsing through the books on color and painting.

Within minutes, Kristy showed Mary Anne a bedroom layout she liked. "This is cool," she remarked. I leaned over to see. To me, it looked more like an office with a sleeping loft in it.

"You could get so much done in a room like this," Kristy said enthusiastically. "These dressers are like filing cabinets, and here's desk space for a computer."

Mary Anne and I stared down at the picture. It was all gray, black, and white, with a splash of red here and there.

"It's kind of . . . cold looking," Mary Anne said.

"Cold?" Kristy took the book back. "It's not cold, it's efficient. There's no wasted space."

"And no color," I added. Mary Anne is already an organized person. But she's also sensitive and warm. I couldn't see her in such an officelike room.

"What are you talking about? There's red in it. And who says black, white, and gray aren't colors?"

Mary Anne shook her head. "It's very tasteful

and sensible," she allowed. "But it's not my style."

Kristy sighed.

The three of us went back to perusing our books. After a minute or so I came across a room I'd love to have. It was navy blue and yellow with cool street signs all over the walls. "How about this?" I suggested, sliding the book to Mary Anne.

Kristy leaned over to see too. I could tell from her skeptical expression she wasn't impressed by it.

Again, Mary Anne shook her head. "I can see you in that room, but not me. Though I do like the colors."

Kristy and I came up with several more rooms that Mary Anne didn't like. Then, finally, she found one herself. A cottage-style bedroom with sheer curtains, a garden mural covering the wall, and a bed with a headboard that looked like a white picket fence. There were lots of built-in cabinets and shelves all trimmed in Mary Anne's two favorite colors, navy blue and yellow.

Kristy just shrugged, but I liked it. At least for Mary Anne. It suited her sweet personality.

Mary Anne showed Sharon the picture. "That doesn't seem too difficult to do," Sharon commented. She put down the book she'd been looking at. "In here they show you how to sponge-paint clouds, which might fit in with your mural. I know a woman who paints murals and does that kind of work. We can call her if you like."

"Awesome!" Mary Anne cried. "This will be great!"

"It'll be pretty," Sharon agreed. "Okay, let's keep looking for curtains and bedding and things like that."

We bought the interior design book and headed upstairs to a store loaded with towels, curtains, bedding, and rugs.

The rugs hung on huge racks. "We'll be putting in hardwood floors, so you'll need an area rug," Sharon said. "Why don't you look through these while I go buy a shower gift I need for tomorrow?"

We began swinging the rugs forward, checking out each design. "Oh, guess what," Kristy said as the three of us stood staring at a floral patterned rug. "I just remembered something."

"What?" Mary Anne and I said together.

"I meant to tell you, Stacey. I saw Wes, that student teacher you were so crazy about. He was in school on Friday."

"I know," I told her. "He's applying for Mr. Z.'s job. I invited him to the party."

"Ooohooh," Mary Anne and Kristy sang.

"You guys! Why shouldn't I invite him? He knows Mr. Zizmore. He might even be my new math teacher."

"Oooohhhhh!"

I thumped Kristy on the shoulder. "Come on. I'm not interested in him anymore."

Kristy pushed another rug forward, one with a cluster of roses in the center of a blue background. "Oh, not much! Like you wouldn't just love to sit around discussing the area of a triangle with Wes." She pitched her voice higher, pretending to be me. "Oh, Wes darling, isn't this a lovely isosceles triangle? Which do you prefer, this or the trapezoid shape?"

Then she lowered her voice, pretending to be Wes. "I can't look now, Stacey my love. I'm calculating the square root of every number ever named."

Mary Anne giggled. "How romantic."

"It might be better than talking to some guy who could only talk about sports," I said.

"Like Logan," Mary Anne muttered.

I suddenly wished I hadn't said that. "No, I didn't mean him," I said. "Plus, he likes other things besides sports."

"What's wrong with sports?" Kristy chimed in indignantly. She's crazy about anything athletic. She even coaches a little-kids' softball team.

"Nothing," I said. "It's just that it's all some guys ever talk about."

"Logan was like that every once in awhile," Mary Anne said. "I tried to be interested since it was so important to him. Sometimes, though, it bored me to death."

"Do you still think about him a lot?" I asked.

She sighed and nodded. "I don't *want* to think about him, but he always seems to pop into my head."

"Maybe it's just a habit," I suggested.

"Or maybe you shouldn't have broken up with him in the first place," Kristy said. We were all friendly with Logan. But Kristy, more than anyone else, thought Mary Anne was nuts for ending things with such a great guy.

"Sometimes it's hard to believe things are over between you two," I said.

"They definitely are," Mary Anne insisted. "Logan was my boyfriend for so long that I'm enjoying being on my own. I like not having to care about what Logan would think about things, or how he'd feel or what he'd like to do. I only have to care about how I feel or what I want."

"That sounds sort of selfish," Kristy remarked.

"Oh, come on!" I cried. "Mary Anne deserves to think about herself once in awhile. She always thinks about other people."

Mary Anne looked at me, surprised. "Thanks," she said.

"You're welcome. And don't be so surprised. If you don't already know that you're one of the nicest people in the world, you should."

She looked even more surprised.

"It's true," Kristy agreed. "And you're entitled to think about yourself if you want to. You shouldn't let guys suck up all your attention."

"That's for sure," I commented. Lately, it seemed that guys were taking over my whole world.

"Speaking of guys," I said, flipping to the next rug, "do you think I should let Toby come visit?"

"No!" Kristy cried.

"Yes," Mary Anne said at the same time, their voices overlapping.

"Not after the way he treated you," Kristy insisted.

"That was awhile ago. People change," said Mary Anne.

"I don't think they do."

"Of course they do. I feel like I'm changing a lot these days."

"Yeah, but you're still basically you."

The two of them continued to argue about whether or not people can change. They pretty much lost sight of the Toby problem.

Sharon returned and suggested we go to the food court to eat. It was a little early for lunch, but she was probably thinking about my diabetes and wanting to make sure I didn't get hungry.

After lunch, we headed home. Sharon dropped me off in front of my house. I went inside, still thinking about Toby. After all, it was only polite to give him some sort of reply. It had been an entire week since I'd received his letter. It wasn't right to put him off forever.

I said hi to Mom, then went to the corner of the living room where the computer sat. I logged on to the Internet and typed in Tobythegreat. The problem was, I still didn't know what I wanted to say to him.

Here's what I wrote:

Hi. It's me, Stacey. I was so surprised to hear from you. Shocked, really. How have you been? I'm fine. I'm busy planning a party for my math teacher, who is moving to Texas. Today I helped Mary Anne shop for new bedroom furnishings.

Since Toby knew Mary Anne from Sea City, I told him about the fire. I didn't mention that she'd broken up with Logan, since that was none of his business.

I typed a pretty long message, then sent it off. There was one other thing I didn't mention in the e-mail — whether I wanted him to visit me.

❋ Chapter 8

On Sunday it snowed again. Watching the flakes fall reminded me that I'd walked through the snow with Ethan just the week before.

It made me miss him.

I picked up the phone to call him. Then I put it down.

What if a call like that gave Ethan the wrong idea about our relationship? I didn't want him to think I was trying to get back together with him.

No. Calling him again so soon would give the wrong impression. I decided against it.

Instead, I went to the window and gazed at the falling snow. At that very moment, my friend Rachel Griffin walked by. She had recently moved into my neighborhood and we liked each another right away.

She used to live in London and wants to be an actress. We have lots in common.

I rapped on the window to get her attention. She waved and turned up our walkway. I hurried to the front hall closet for my jacket. I was putting it on as the doorbell rang.

"Where are you headed?" I asked Rachel.

"Nowhere." I noticed she was wearing her beautiful dark hair in two braids. She looked relaxed and happy. Like a person going nowhere and enjoying it.

"Want some company?" I asked.

"Yeah. Definitely."

I didn't have to be anywhere until four-thirty. That's when Jeremy and I had arranged to meet and go to the mall for dinner and a movie. My mother had agreed to drive us.

I called to Mom that I was going out. "Where are you headed?" she yelled from the kitchen.

"Nowhere," I shouted back as I went out the front door.

Rachel and I walked around the neighborhood, enjoying the snow and talking. I discussed my Ethan problem with her. "How much time should you spend with a guy who's your friend but no longer your boyfriend?" I asked.

I knew Rachel had a close guy friend back in London.

"I don't know," she replied. "It's tricky. Boys get the wrong idea so easily. E-mail helps."

"What do you mean?"

"When you leave an e-mail message, it's almost like writing a letter. Your friend can get back to you when he's ready, and you can do the same. Somehow it's not as personal as talking over the phone."

I hadn't thought of it like that. But it made sense. E-mail didn't demand your instant attention the way the phone did. And you had time to think about your responses.

"But what if you miss the person and want to hear his voice?" I asked. Frankly, that's how I was feeling about Ethan that afternoon.

Rachel shrugged. "I didn't say it was perfect."

We walked for about forty-five minutes more, until the cold made us shiver. Then we went to Rachel's house and watched a video.

When I stepped back inside my house, I took off my jacket and sat at the computer. I'd decided to take Rachel's advice and e-mail Ethan — stay in touch by computer. Logging onto the Internet, I received an instant message almost immediately.

It was from Tobythegreat.

Hi, Stacey, he wrote. *Wow, was I glad to hear from you. After awhile I was afraid you really hated me or something and that you'd never answer. Anyway, how's everything? What a bummer about Mary Anne's house.*

I composed an answer right away. I didn't have that much to say. I wrote that it was snowing, and more about Mr. Z. leaving and what a great teacher he was.

But I'd still avoided the important question: Could Toby come visit?

I noticed that he hadn't brought it up again either. I was impressed that he had that much self-control. " 'Bye." I wrote and clicked off the instant message box.

Next I started an e-mail to Ethan. *Hi, Ethan,* I began. *Can you believe it's been a whole week since New Year's? Actually, so much has happened that it seems like a long time —*

I was interrupted by electronic chimes.

Toby again.

Too bad about your teacher leaving, he wrote. *One hard thing about starting high school is you don't know who the good teachers are and which ones are duds. Kids try to tell you but they don't always agree.*

The more I read, the more it seemed Toby had turned into a pretty cool guy. Mom always says that boys take awhile to mature, that they mature later than girls. Maybe he'd finally matured, at least a little.

I wrote him back. Instantly I received a reply.

In this note, he finally mentioned the visit. *I'd still like to come see you, if that would be okay. I kind of need an answer because Dad has to work the detour into his schedule. He's a maniac about schedules — you don't even want to know how weird he is on the subject.*

Okay. It wasn't fair of me to put him off any longer.

Sure. Drop by when you're in town, I wrote. I hoped that made it sound casual, not like some big event or date.

Excellent! he wrote. *I'll see you next Saturday. 'Bye!* He logged off.

Staring at the screen, I had a sinking feeling. Something was wrong.

Suddenly, I realized what it was.

Saturday! Mr. Z.'s party was on Saturday!

"What's the matter, Stacey?" Mom asked. I hadn't even heard her come into the living room. "You look panicked."

"Remember that guy Toby I told you about? I

just e-mailed him that he could come visit. He e-mailed me back that he was coming on Saturday, the same day as the party."

"Write him back and say that's not a good time," Mom suggested calmly.

"It's the only time he can come," I said. "It's when his parents are passing through this way."

"Then I suppose he can't come," Mom said.

"I'd feel dumb telling him that now." Besides, after reading his messages, I was interested in seeing him again.

"Well," Mom began, considering. "Do you know what time he's coming? Maybe you could see him during the day, before the party."

"You're right!" I cried. "I bet he's planning to come during the day."

"Write him that you're busy in the evening, but you'd love to see him in the afternoon."

"Cool," I said. Turning back to the computer, I began typing an e-mail telling Toby that the Mr. Z. party was that night, but it would be great if he could come in the afternoon.

I signed off the Internet, feeling much better.

By five o'clock, Jeremy and I were standing in line to buy tickets at the movie theater at Washington

Mall. We'd decided on a comedy that was actually a remake of a TV show from the 1960s.

"How was sledding?" I asked him.

He'd been gazing around the mall. Now he turned to me as if my voice had startled him. "Huh?"

"Sledding," I reminded him. "You went yesterday. How was it?"

He smiled and a light seemed to go on in his amazing green-flecked brown eyes. "Oh, great. My cousins are from Atlanta and it doesn't snow much down there, so they were really having a great time. They're crazy guys, but fun."

"Maybe I can meet them sometime."

"Yeah. For sure." He glanced away again.

"Are you searching for something in particular?" I asked him.

"Not really," he replied with an uncomfortable laugh. "Just checking around for anyone I might know."

I wasn't thrilled with his answer. He probably was looking for someone in particular. And even if he wasn't, was I so boring?

I didn't want to start an argument, though. So I let it pass.

The ticket booth opened and the line began moving forward quickly. It wasn't long before we were seated in the theater.

The movie was hysterical. At each joke, I turned toward Jeremy to share the laugh, but he seemed to be daydreaming. Either he didn't think the movie was funny, or he wasn't even paying attention to it.

After the movie, we headed for the food court for supper.

"What did you think of the movie?" I asked.

"It was okay. Not my favorite."

It bugged me a little that he hadn't liked the movie. I'd thought it was great. Of course, I was being silly. I knew that he didn't have to like it just because I did. Still . . .

"Is something the matter?" I asked.

"No. Why?"

"You seem sort of distracted."

"I do?"

I nodded. We walked to the center of the court and gazed at the choices. "What are you in the mood to eat?" I asked.

He shrugged. "Whatever. I don't care."

"Jeremy, it isn't me, is it? I mean, are you okay with our relationship? You still want to go out, don't you?"

His brow wrinkled into a confused expression. "Sure I do. What makes you think I don't?"

"It's that faraway look you have."

"I just don't care what we eat," he insisted. "Maybe I'm tired from sledding yesterday. We were on the hill for seven hours."

"I guess that must be it. How about eating at Wok 'N' Roll?"

"Fine."

As we walked toward the Chinese take-out stand, I still couldn't get past the feeling that something about Jeremy just wasn't right.

❋ Chapter 9

Stacey McGill and Peter Black, please report to the front office.

The announcement came over the PA system within the first five minutes of homeroom on Monday morning.

"Uh-oh," kids in my class teased as I stood up to leave.

My teacher nodded to me, and I headed into the hall. I wasn't too nervous. Since the school secretary, Mrs. Downey, had also called Pete, I assumed it was about the party.

As I walked down the hall, though, I began worrying. Had something gone wrong with the party?

I met Pete in front of the office. "Do you know what this is about?" I asked him.

"No. The party probably." He didn't look worried.

Inside, Mrs. Downey smiled at us. "Someone dropped your party sign-up sheet off here," she said, handing me the paper. "Also, Mr. Kingbridge would like to speak to you."

While we waited, I looked over the paper. "Lots of kids signed up," I observed.

"That's good, because if we start inviting old students, this is going to be a huge party," Pete pointed out.

I nodded, feeling a little tickle of worry. Did we have enough time to pull the party together? Was it getting too big?

Mrs. Downey nodded to us. "Mr. Kingbridge will see you now." We got up and went into his office.

"I just wanted to bring you up to date," Mr. Kingbridge said from behind his desk. "I've spoken to a few people, and we can cover your decorating costs. Just keep receipts for everything you buy and you'll be paid back. Also, the head of the alumni committee will contact Mr. Zizmore's former students and invite them. So you don't have to be concerned about doing that. Teachers have set up their first planning meeting for Tuesday. Why don't you students do the same. That way if anyone wants to help the teachers they can volunteer then. Also, you can touch base with the teachers."

"Great," I said. "It's still a surprise, isn't it?"

"So far, no one has spilled the beans," he assured me.

Pete and I spread the word that our first planning meeting would be held in the lunchroom after school on Tuesday.

"Can Sam come too?" Kristy asked me at lunch that afternoon. Sam is her fifteen-year-old brother. He'd had Mr. Z. for math.

I knew this because Sam was one of the first guys I'd ever dated. Believe it or not, we talked about math a lot when we were out together.

"Sam is in the math club now, and he says if it weren't for Mr. Z. he'd never have discovered how much fun math can be," Kristy continued.

Claudia let out a sharp, disbelieving laugh. "Math? Fun?"

"It can be," I said, speaking to her for the first time in awhile. (I was trying to act on my New Year's resolution and be a better friend — one who could patch things up.)

"I suppose it has a use for you. It helps you keep

track of all your old boyfriends," she snapped back at me.

I shot her a disgusted look. Why had I wanted to be friends with her again? At that moment, I couldn't remember.

Her nasty remark made me think, though. I did seem to have accumulated a lot of ex-boyfriends. And, for some reason, they all seemed to be appearing, or reappearing, this week.

What was it? Had my planets suddenly lined up in some romance formation?

And — I wondered — was it normal to have so many ex-boyfriends at thirteen?

Oh, well. What was there to say? I like boys and I've never had trouble finding a boy who liked me.

"Uh-oh," Kristy muttered in a voice just loud enough for those of us sitting at the table to hear. "Look who's coming over here."

Glancing over my shoulder, I saw Rachel walking toward us.

Kristy slumped down in her seat.

Claudia opened her English textbook and stared down at the pages of Shakespeare as if she were fascinated.

Mary Anne wrung her hands, while Abby bit down on an amused smile.

Abby's and my friends knew Rachel from before I moved to Stoneybrook. And it was an understatement to say that they hadn't liked her. She'd moved away in the fifth grade, to London. I'd never heard of her until she returned to Stoneybrook. Neither had Abby.

Whatever she'd been like then didn't mean anything to me. I thought she was great. But my friends couldn't forget the old Rachel.

"You guys," I said under my breath.

"Make her go away," Kristy said teasingly.

"Hi, Rachel," I said when she arrived at the table.

"Hi," she replied. "Hi, everyone."

At least my friends all forced a smile.

"Stacey, I wanted to know if I could sign up to help with the party, even though I don't have Mr. Zizmore for a teacher," she said.

"Sure," I answered. "We're having a meeting after school tomorrow. Right here."

"Terrific. I'll see you then."

"I can't believe you're going to let her be on your committee," Kristy muttered as Rachel walked away.

"Why not?" I asked.

"She'll find some way to wreck it."

"That's for double sure," Claudia agreed.

I just rolled my eyes.

At other times — before this — I'd tried convincing them that Rachel had changed. They didn't even want to consider it.

"What about Sam?" Kristy reminded me. "Can he help? I mean, you let Rachel and Jeremy join and they never even had Mr. Zizmore for a teacher."

"Sure," I agreed. "Why not? Anyone who wants to can help out."

That evening I had a baby-sitting job for the Hill family. Sara and Norman had colds and went to bed early. I spent the rest of the time making notes for the party meeting the next day.

When I got home, Mom told me she'd noticed I had some e-mail waiting for me. Before anything else, I logged on to the Internet.

Hi, it's me, Toby. Saturday during the day is great. I'm not exactly sure when I'll arrive. But Dad, the schedule freak, will have it narrowed down by Friday. I'll call you and let you know. I'll need your phone number, though. E-mail it to me before Thursday.

I can't wait to see you. I've been remembering the wonderful times we had at Sea City. And our kiss. It's my fault that we had only one. Maybe I can make up for that when I see you. Toby.

I leaned away from the computer as if Toby were about to jump out of it and grab me.

A kiss!

He was planning to kiss me?

This wasn't what I had in mind. Not at all.

By Tuesday afternoon I was feeling pretty nervous about the meeting.

"Don't worry about it," Pete said as we headed toward the cafeteria together. "This is just the first meeting. We can check in with the teachers and figure out who will do what on the decorating and invitations."

"Hey! Stacey!" I turned and saw Jeremy hurrying toward me.

I introduced him to Pete. Jeremy was polite but a little cold to Pete. Well, more distant than cold, really.

The three of us continued walking toward the lunchroom.

"How should we open the meeting?" Pete asked.

"We could ask people for decorating ideas," I suggested.

"Stacey, want to go downtown after school with me Thursday?" Jeremy said. "I thought we could hang out, maybe even eat there. Claudia was telling me the Rosebud Cafe is good."

Before I could answer, Pete jumped in. "I think we should see if any kids want to work with the teachers, then see who's left."

I didn't know who to reply to first!

There was a competition for my attention going on here — and I didn't know how to deal with it.

"Hang on," I said, trying to sound light.

"Sure, we can talk to them all together first," I said to Pete.

I turned toward Jeremy. "I think I can go downtown Thursday. It depends how this meeting goes, I suppose."

I saw Robert coming down the hall toward us.

We stopped to wait for him.

He and Pete did a high five.

Then I introduced Robert to Jeremy. "He just moved here from Olympia, Washington," I explained.

"Hi," Robert said, but his voice wasn't friendly. I wondered if he was aware that Jeremy and I were going out now. From the suspicious way he eyed Jeremy, I had the feeling he knew.

The four of us entered the cafeteria together. About twenty kids were already scattered among the closest tables. The teachers were meeting at the far end of the lunchroom. "Thanks for coming, everybody," I said loudly. "We can start now. Come on over here."

The kids gathered around. Pete didn't make a move to say anything. I wasn't sure where to start, so I plunged right in. First I sent any kids who didn't want to work on decorations or invitations over to help the teachers. Then I turned the talk to decorating.

"I thought Texas might be a good theme, since that's where Mr. Z. is going," I began. "Anyone else have any ideas?"

Not surprisingly, Kristy had one. "How about memories — stuff we can dig up from the past that relates to Mr. Zizmore."

"Too hard to do," Grace Blume disagreed. "We only have less than a week. How about a math theme?"

"That's what I was thinking," Pete added.

"Not too exciting," Jeremy objected.

"It would be exciting to Mr. Z.," Robert shot back in an annoyed tone. I wasn't sure if he was bugged because Jeremy disagreed with Pete, who was Robert's friend, or if Robert just didn't like Jeremy on account of me.

Sam, Kristy's brother, hurried in. "Sorry I'm late," he said.

"That's okay," I replied, smiling at him. "Got any ideas for a theme?"

"Bon voyage?" he said, more as a question than a statement.

The group groaned, but Sam just laughed. "I guess not," he said.

We threw around some other ideas. Future Math, with a space theme. Rachel suggested Great Math Minds, with pictures of Euclid, Pythagoras, Sir Isaac Newton, and Einstein hanging alongside pictures of Mr. Zizmore.

By a show of hands, we settled on Great Math Minds.

Before I could think about it much more, Wes walked into the lunchroom.

My breath caught sharply in my throat.

He read my surprised expression and explained. "I've asked to help you on this. Mr. Zizmore's guidance really meant a lot to me."

I suddenly felt very self-conscious with Wes observing me.

"Does anyone have any idea where we'll find pictures of these great mathematicians?" I asked the group.

Everyone sat there, staring blankly.

"We desperately need Claudia's help," Jeremy said.

I looked at him, surprised. He was right, of course. Claudia is the creative one who always put the extra artistic touch into projects like this. She could probably even draw the pictures herself.

Still . . .

I couldn't believe he'd said it. He knows Claudia and I are fighting. Wasn't I doing a good enough job? Weren't things moving along just fine without her?

It seemed so disloyal.

On the other hand . . .

She would be a great person to head this group. If I told her that, she'd be flattered. It might give us an excuse to end our fight.

✿ Chapter 10

I spent most of Wednesday thinking about approaching Claudia to talk. Our fight had gone on for so long. It made me nervous about opening things up. But Claudia and I had been best friends for much longer than we'd been enemies. Why should I feel so awkward about talking to someone I used to tell *everything* to?

Still, I tried talking to her during lunch, but I couldn't do it. Too public. Besides, Kristy surprised me with a bit of news I hadn't expected.

"At dinner last night, Sam went on and on about how great you looked yesterday," she informed me. "Look out, Stacey. I think he's in love again."

"You're joking!"

She shook her head. "I'm not. After the meeting

he wouldn't stop talking about you. It practically ruined my dinner."

"Thanks a lot," I told her wryly. "But I hardly even spoke to him."

"Sam doesn't fall in love through his ears," Kristy said. "He falls in love with what he sees. And you looked good to him yesterday."

Claudia let out a disdainful little snort — meant as an insult, I was sure.

I just stared at her and then turned away.

Maybe I didn't want to be friends again after all.

I left the lunchroom that day with boys on my mind.

Did Kristy's bombshell mean I had to deal with Sam now? If it had come at another time, I might have been flattered. But right now, I didn't need *another* guy from my past hovering around.

Maybe it was something about the new year. First I'd resolved to contact Ethan. Then Toby had popped up out of nowhere. Next, Pete and I wound up working on the party together. Then Robert — who had barely wanted to participate in anything since the last time I saw him — suddenly decided this was the time to get involved. Adding to that, Wes, my big crush, had returned. Now Sam. And I couldn't forget Jeremy.

It was too much!

Thinking about all of them was giving me a headache.

Ordinarily, I'd have run all this past Claudia. She was good at helping me sort through things. We might even have shared a few laughs over it.

No — we'd *definitely* have laughed.

It's not as easy to see the humor in things by yourself.

After school I met some kids from my committee. We went shopping for decoration supplies. It didn't take long. I was still able to arrive at Claudia's house around four-thirty, an hour before our Wednesday BSC meeting was to begin. (BSC is short for Baby-sitters Club. It's a sitting business. Clients call us during meetings to arrange for sitters for their kids.)

I'd made a decision.

I was going to talk to Claudia even if it — or she — killed me.

I entered Claudia's house and went straight upstairs to her room. I never used to knock on her bedroom door, but today I did.

"Come in," Claudia called.

When I stepped inside, she was stretched across her bed, sketching in her pad. She glanced up at me casually, and then her face changed as if she'd just seen Frankenstein's monster appear in her room. A look of complete panic swept across her face. She flipped her sketch pad shut and sat straight up. Her eyes darted to the clock on her dresser. "It's not five-thirty yet," she said.

"I know. I came to talk to you."

"About what?"

I drew in a long, shaky breath. There were so many things. Our fight. Boys.

"About Mr. Z.'s party," I said instead. "We really need your help."

"No, you don't. I saw that list. You have lots of help."

"But no one else has your artistic talent," I insisted. "We need you to help with decorations."

I was about to tell her that Jeremy agreed with me, had even been the first to suggest it — but I couldn't make myself bring up his name.

"You want me to do artwork?" she asked.

I nodded. "We need portraits of great mathematicians. A picture of Mr. Zizmore. And anything else your creative mind can come up with."

"I'd need a photo of Mr. Zizmore," she said

thoughtfully. "There's probably one in last year's yearbook."

"We can find you the other pictures," I suggested. "They don't have to be paintings. Just big black-and-white sketches."

"Who else is helping out?" she asked.

"Lots of good kids," I replied. Somehow, I just couldn't bring up the name *Jeremy*. Things were going too well to spoil them now by reminding her of him. And it didn't seem a good idea to mention Rachel either. I figured the answer I gave her was true enough.

"Okay," she said. "I'll do it."

"Oh, that's great, thanks," I cried. Normally, I would have hugged her, but I couldn't. Not yet.

"One more thing," I said.

"What?"

I took a deep breath. "I just hate that we've been fighting. I'm sorry for the rotten things I've said to you. I didn't mean them. I'd really like for us to be friends again."

There. I'd said it.

Her face was blank.

I could feel my heart beating.

"Me too," she said finally.

A smile broke out on my face. "Really?"

"Yes," she said. "I'm sorry for the way I've been acting too."

Again, it seemed like a moment to hug. But somehow we couldn't get that far. Not yet.

We did smile at each other, though.

Kristy burst through the door. "Hey, Claudia, what do you think of this — "

She stopped short, staring at us. "Hey. Are you guys actually smiling at each other?"

Claudia stopped smiling.

Then she started again.

"I guess so," she admitted.

"Definitely," I said.

Mary Anne arrived then. She looked from Claudia to me and broke into a wide smile of her own.

The four of us must have looked pretty goofy — standing there, grinning at one another.

I didn't care, though.

"Well, let's start this meeting," Kristy suggested after another moment of smiling.

On Claudia's desk I noticed my plate of raw veggies, the one Claudia makes for me at every meeting. She'd spread them out artistically today. (At the last few meetings she'd simply thrown them down on a plate or shoved them, still in the cellophane bag, at me.) I took this to mean she'd wanted to make things better between us too.

There was still so much we needed to talk about. Jeremy — for one thing.

But this was a good start.

❀ Chapter 11

Claudia knelt on the lunchroom floor, working intently. "Who has the photo of Einstein? I'm ready for it."

It was Thursday afternoon, and our committee was hard at work. Claudia had jumped into the project with all the natural enthusiasm she brings to anything art-related.

"I have it," Jeremy told her. I watched as he hurried to her side with a fresh sheet of poster board and a black-and-white picture of Albert Einstein he'd photocopied from a book. (He and I had postponed our Rosebud Cafe date because there was so much to do for the party.)

He picked up the poster board she'd just finished. "Isaac Newton. Awesome!" he cried.

"Does it really look like him?" Claudia asked, smiling.

"I'd know him anywhere!" Jeremy replied.

"Yeah. I'm sure you'd know Sir Isaac Newton if you bumped into him."

"I would! He'd be the guy in the breeches with the bump on his head from where the apple hit him."

"I guess he would stand out in a crowd," Claudia agreed, grinning.

Rachel appeared beside me. "Does that bother you?" she said quietly.

"What?" I asked.

"You know what."

"Jeremy and Claudia?" Up until that point I hadn't been bothered. At least, not that I was aware of. I'd been watching them, without making much of it.

"You know she'd like to grab him for herself," Rachel said.

"I don't know. They're friends. No one ever said they couldn't be. It would be pretty pathetic if I got upset with Jeremy just for talking to her."

"I don't know," Rachel said in a singsongy voice, studying Claudia, who had started work on her Einstein sketch. Jeremy sat cross-legged on the floor beside her and held the photo up for her to check.

"I'm not going to worry about it," I said. "Would you come with me? I need you to help me cut out some of the numbers we're going to hang up."

"Sure," Rachel agreed. "I just have to say, I admire your trust. You certainly don't *act* upset anyway."

We walked to the table where sheets of silver oak tag with huge stenciled numbers had been laid out. I didn't know who'd made them, but they looked great.

"Thanks," I said to Rachel. "But I'm really *not* upset about Claudia and Jeremy, so why should I act upset?"

"No reason."

I stared hard at Rachel. I didn't like the tone of her voice. She was wrong about Jeremy and Claudia.

Wasn't she?

On Friday afternoon, as we were headed to the lunchroom to work on the party, Mr. Kingbridge stopped Pete and me. "Everything's set for Saturday," he told us. "My wife and I will show up here at school with Mr. and Mrs. Zizmore at six o'clock. I'll pretend to accidentally hit the horn when I pull up. That will be your signal to turn out the lights and hide."

"Perfect!" I said.

"Okay, see you tomorrow," said Mr. Kingbridge, hurrying off. Then he stopped and turned back. "One of you should prepare a speech."

"I think we're in good shape," Pete commented as Mr. Kingbridge walked away. "Claudia was a big help. Did you straighten things out with her? It looks as if you two have stopped fighting."

"We have. And I'm so happy. Hey, listen, who's going to make the speech?"

"You. Definitely. I can't talk in public."

"Well . . . okay."

"It's been great working with you, Stacey," said Pete.

Uh-oh. That sounded like the introduction to a mushy moment. I liked Pete, but I didn't want him to get the wrong idea.

"I've enjoyed it too," I answered in the most friendly, unromantic voice I could manage. "It's been fun." I looked at my watch. "We'd better get to the meeting."

"Yeah," said Pete, looking — and sounding — disappointed.

When we arrived at the cafeteria, work was moving along without us. Claudia was filling in her great mathematicians sketches with pastels. Her last drawing, the one of Mr. Zizmore, was awesome. It looked just like him.

The teachers' music committee had brought in a great sound system, borrowed from someone's restaurant. They were busy unpacking it. The food committee was moving tables and setting out foil trays of plastic utensils.

Robert ran in from the back door. "He's gone!" he announced. "His car just pulled out of the parking lot."

Pete turned to me. "I put Robert on Mr. Z. watch," he explained. "Now that he's gone for the day, we can officially start setting up."

"I can't believe this was his last day as our teacher," I said. "He looked so sad in class today. I almost cried."

"Hopefully the party will cheer him up," Pete replied.

He walked to the center of the cafeteria. "Okay, everybody, set up as much as you can," he said. "We have to leave here by five o'clock today so the custodians can mop the floor, but they'll open the building for us around three tomorrow. We can finish up then."

Tomorrow. Saturday. I'd e-mailed my phone number to Toby and had calmed down about the kiss thing.

To be honest, I was starting to feel excited about his visit. Maybe Toby had outgrown all the traits I'd disliked about him and kept only the good ones. After all, his e-mails had been pretty interesting. And what if he'd grown into a hunk since the last time I saw him? It was possible.

Maybe by the end of the day, I'd *want* him to kiss me.

I glanced at Jeremy, who was — once again — helping Claudia.

What was I thinking? Was it right to be so excited about seeing an old boyfriend when you already had a perfectly nice current one?

Somehow I didn't think it was. What did it mean?

Probably nothing. It just meant I hadn't seen Toby in awhile. He was something new to be excited about.

That's what I told myself. But I couldn't get over

the feeling that something about my reaction to his visit wasn't the way it should be.

On Saturday morning, Mom called me to the phone at nine-thirty. "It's me, Toby. I'm calling from the cellular. We're on the road." He sounded in a great mood.

"Hi. Are you still coming?" I asked.

"How about if I crash-land on you at about eleven-thirty this morning?"

"Okay. Sure."

"I'll stay until the 'rents come back for me around two."

"The *rents*?"

"Pa-*rents*," he explained.

"Oh," I said with a light laugh. "Okay. Do you have the directions I e-mailed you?"

"Got 'em right here. See you soon, babe."

He clicked off.

Babe?

I stood staring at the phone in my hand.

Babe?

Oh, well, I thought as I hung up. It sounded as if he was just in a silly, happy kind of mood. He was only being flip and upbeat.

The phone rang again. "Hello?" I said.

"Hi, it's Jeremy. Do you feel like doing something before we go over to the school later?"

"I would. But . . . um . . . I can't."

"How come?"

My mind raced. Should I tell him the truth? No. Yes. No. Yes.

"An old friend is going to be visiting. From out of state. My friend Toby."

"Cool. When's the last time you saw her?"

"A *long* time ago," I answered.

Her. Jeremy thought Toby was a her. Would it be a lie to let him go on thinking that?

"I'll see you at school, though," I said. "Maybe we can do something afterward."

"All right. Have fun with Toby."

"Thanks."

I showered quickly and dressed, settling on jeans, a black velvet long-sleeved T-shirt, and my boots. I put on some tinted lip gloss but no other makeup.

At eleven-thirty — sharp — the bell rang. I recalled that Toby had said his father was a schedule freak, so I wasn't surprised that he was right on time.

When I reached the front door, Mom was already there, opening it.

I saw Toby standing in the doorway.

He was so . . . the same.

Exactly the same as I remembered him.

"Hi, Toby," I said. "Come on in."

He turned and waved in the direction of a station wagon parked at the curb. The driver — his dad, I guessed — honked and pulled away.

"Mom, this is Toby," I said.

"Hello," she replied. She seemed a little suspicious of him, but he didn't seem to notice.

"Hey, nice house," he commented, looking right at home as he wandered into the living room. "And there's the old e-mailer," he added, pointing to the computer.

Mom asked if he was hungry.

"Just downed a half-dozen doughnuts on the way here," he said. He put a fisted hand to his chest. For a moment I thought he would belch. He only pounded his chest lightly, though.

He looked at me and grinned. "I think you got taller," he said. "You look great. How about me?" He squared his shoulders proudly. "I'm not the same guy you remember, am I?"

Exactly the same, I thought again. He'd been cute to begin with. But I'd expected him to seem older now. Be taller. Something.

"You look good too," I replied.

"Can you tell I've been working out?"

Had he really come all this way to show me his muscles? I was relieved he didn't flex his arm or something.

"You have such a big sweater on," I commented. "It's hard to tell."

He pulled out the bottom hem of his sweater as if he'd forgotten he was wearing it. "I guess so," he said. "But, yeah. I've been pumping since the summer. Believe me. It shows."

"I'm sure it must," I said politely. I hoped the conversation was going to improve after this. Maybe Toby was just floundering a little — feeling awkward or something.

We sat down on the couch. "Have you seen any interesting colleges?" I asked.

"Not really. Besides, college isn't for me. I'm going to join some branch of the military. Army. Navy. I'm not sure yet."

"Oh. That could be interesting, I guess."

"Definitely."

"Would you like to go for a walk, see the neighborhood?" I suggested. I was hoping a walk might help us both relax.

"Okay," he agreed.

I grabbed my jacket and we headed outside. It was bitterly cold. I immediately wanted to turn around and go back inside. But I didn't know what else to do with Toby.

Worse, I couldn't even think of anything much to say. The funny thing was that Toby didn't seem to mind — or notice. He talked about himself, his school, his future in the military.

The more he talked, the more I realized that we had almost nothing in common. And the less I could think of to say in reply. I even wondered if someone else had written his e-mails for him.

I began secretly checking my watch, hoping two o'clock would come quickly.

We went back inside and I fixed us some toaster pizzas for lunch. Glancing at the clock, I saw that it was one-thirty. My mood brightened. Only one more half-hour of Toby and then I'd be free. No doubt his father would be pulling up at two on the dot.

Thank goodness.

"It's too bad you have to go so soon," I said, offering him another piece of pizza. "But it works out, because I have to go to school to help set up the party I told you about." I chatted on about the party.

At two, both of us looked at the clock at the same time. "Mr. Punctual should be honking the horn right now," Toby said.

We listened. No honk.

"Your clock must be wrong." Toby stood up from the table. "I might as well put on my coat."

"Okay." I walked him to the front hall and found his jacket.

"This was really great, Stacey," he said. "Even though we didn't do anything, it was fun."

Didn't do anything? I wondered what he'd expected. Did he think I was planning entertainment for his visit? "I'm sorry if you thought we were going to do something," I said.

"No, I said it was fine." But his tone let me know he was disappointed.

Well, what did I care? At that point I only wanted him to leave, so I could get on with my life.

The doorbell rang.

Toby's eyes widened with surprise. "Hey, you rate! Dad walked all the way to the door."

He leaned forward and took hold of my arm. I saw that he expected a good-bye kiss.

I couldn't. I just couldn't. Instead, I reached behind me and swung the door open.

My sudden movement threw Toby off balance,

sending him tottering into me, knocking me into the doorjamb.

I turned my head to see Toby's father.

But it wasn't Toby's father.

"Ethan!" I gasped.

✿ Chapter 12

"What are you doing here?" I cried, trying not to sound as panicked as I felt. (I don't think I succeeded.)

"Glad to see me, huh?" Ethan joked. He grinned at me but scowled at Toby. I suppose it must have looked pretty suspicious — my flying out the door and Toby's practically landing on top of me.

"I am! I *am* glad to see you," I said. "Come on in."

Ethan stepped inside. He and Toby stared at each other awkwardly.

"Ethan, this is my friend Toby. He just . . . kind of . . . tripped right then. Toby, this is Ethan." They shook hands quickly.

"I'm here for the art exhibition," Ethan explained.

I blinked at him, my mind a blank.

"My teacher. Remember? At the Stoneybrook Museum?"

"The Stoneybrook Museum! Right! Now I remember."

"I should have called you. It's my fault," Ethan said.

"How do you two know each other?" Toby asked cautiously.

"From the city," Ethan said.

Ethan was great. He didn't even *hint* that we used to date. I thought that was very cool.

"Stacey and I know each other from Sea City," Toby continued. "One of those summer vacation things, if you know what I mean."

Very uncool.

Toby was trying to make it sound as if we were closer than we were. Ethan's expression held steady, though. He didn't seem at all bothered.

"Guys, I have a problem," I told them. And it wasn't that two of my ex-boyfriends were standing face-to-face in my hallway. "I have to be at school by three. I'm sort of in charge of the decorations and the surprise part of this party we're throwing for a teacher who's moving."

The phone rang, and I ran into the kitchen

to pick it up. "Hello. Is Toby there?" said an unfamiliar voice on the other end. "This is his mother."

"Hi. This is Stacey. Sure. Just a minute."

I handed Toby the phone. While he talked to his mother, Ethan took me aside. "Did I put you in a bad spot?" he asked. "I mean with . . . that guy."

"No!" I told him. "No way. He's leaving. Like, forever."

Ethan grinned. "Good."

"But I really do have to go to school soon to help set up."

"Let me think," Ethan said. "I was hoping we'd hang out and then go to the museum. But how about this? I'll go over by myself and meet you later. The only thing is, I have some time to kill beforehand."

"Problemo!" Toby announced, reappearing.

"What?" I asked.

"My brother scored a last-minute campus interview and tour at Yale. Great opportunity. But it means I'm stranded here until it's done."

"Oh, wow," I murmured.

"Yeah," Toby said, looking helpless and a little embarrassed. "Who'd have thought Mr. Schedule would have picked today to develop a little flexibility?"

I held up my index finger. "One minute, okay?"

Calmly, I walked up the stairs. When I hit the second-floor landing, I bolted for my mother's bedroom.

"Mom!" I cried, bursting into her room.

She looked up sharply from the book she'd been reading. "What's wrong?"

"Toby and Ethan are both downstairs and I have to be at school in twenty minutes."

She drew in a long breath. "How did this happen?"

"I forgot Ethan said he might come up, and Toby is supposed to be gone by now, except he's still here. I have to dress for the party. Could you please keep them busy while I do? Pretty please?"

She flipped the book shut and stood up. "I'll do my best. But I don't think they'll exactly be thrilled to hang out with me."

"Sure they will," I assured her. "You can be very entertaining."

"Oh, right," she said with a laugh.

As she headed down the stairs, I bolted into my room to change. I was supposed to give a speech at the party. And I didn't want to look a wreck with everyone staring at me. I didn't have a clear idea of what I would say — just a general idea. Whatever I said, I wanted to look good saying it.

My heart was racing. "Calm down," I commanded myself. Neither of these guys was my boyfriend. I really didn't have to worry about them being together. Ethan was already cool with it. And Toby would have to be cool too.

Feeling a little calmer, I dressed. Fortunately, I'd already picked out what I wanted to wear — the neon-blue dress I hadn't been able to use on New Year's Eve.

I held it out in front of me and wondered if it was a little too dressy. I didn't care, though. I wanted to wear it. I slipped on the dress. Then I did a fast makeup job and added my jewelry. By the time I was finished putting myself together, I was pleased with the result.

Now I had just one problem. Toby and Ethan. What was I going to do with them?

I headed back downstairs, hoping I'd think of something.

"We've solved the problem!" Toby announced, hurrying out of the living room to meet me on the stairs. "We'll go to the party with you!"

"That's if you don't mind," Ethan added quickly.

"I . . . I guess that would be okay," I said.

"I'll leave before it ends and go to the museum,"

Ethan said. "But I need someplace to be until the opening begins."

"We'll help you finish setting up," Toby volunteered.

Was this a good idea? I looked over their heads to check with Mom, who stood in the living room. Her expression was concerned, but she just shrugged. I guessed that meant, *Don't look at me. I don't know.* Apparently this had been the boys' plan, not hers.

"All right," I said. "Let's get going."

I had an awful feeling that taking them with me would only lead to trouble. But I didn't know what else to do.

❀ Chapter 13

We arrived at the school only about ten minutes late. Not everyone had shown up yet. Jeremy hurried to me. "Stacey, you look beautiful," he said.

"Thanks," I replied.

He glanced over my shoulder at Ethan and Toby, who were hanging back awkwardly, hands in pockets, by the door. "Who are those guys?"

"One is my friend Toby and — "

"Toby's a him?"

With a little grimace, I nodded.

"And the other guy?"

This one was even harder. I knew he would recognize Ethan's name. And the idea of Ethan already bugged him.

"Ethan," I revealed in a small, muffled voice.

"Who?"

"Ethan," I said more clearly.

I expected him to freak out and I cringed, waiting for the blast.

"Aren't you going to introduce me?" he asked cheerfully.

"Well, sure," I answered. "They're just friends of mine, you know."

"I know."

I made the introductions. "We could use some help hanging crepe paper," Jeremy said.

"Let me at it," replied Toby. "I'm a crepe paper master."

"I'm no master, but I'll be glad to help," Ethan added.

As the three of them went off together to hang paper, Pete approached me. "Everything's pretty much under control," he said. He stepped back and took in my outfit. "You look great."

"Thanks."

A girl on the food committee rushed across the room to us. "One of the building guys just told us we can't use those little Sterno cans to keep the food warm. He says it's against the fire code."

Pete and I looked at each other. "I'll go talk to him," Pete offered.

Someone tapped me on the shoulder and I turned. It was Wes.

He was wearing jeans and a sweatshirt. I'd never seen him dressed so casually. He looked gorgeous, of course.

He must have noticed that I was staring at him. (How embarrassing.) "Don't worry," he said. "I plan to run home to change before the party."

"Oh." I laughed nervously. "I wasn't worrying about that."

"Do you need anything here, Stacey?" he asked.

"Pete's seeing about a problem with the Sterno," I informed him. "Maybe you could help." I pointed across the room to where Pete spoke with a custodian wearing gray overalls.

"Let me see what I can do," he offered, walking toward them.

Suddenly, a loud shout came from the middle of the room. I saw Toby swinging in midair, clutching a light fixture, a heap of colored crepe paper in a pile beneath him, a ladder toppling in slow motion.

I ran to help Ethan right the ladder, which Toby had accidentally kicked out from under himself.

"The crepe paper master is performing his wizardry," Ethan joked.

There was much more to be done than I'd expected. I wound up finding a white apron in the kitchen and putting it on, just to keep my dress from getting dirty. While I worked I tried to nail down the exact words of the speech I'd give later.

But by five, when teachers, students, and former students began showing up, the place looked spectacular. Claudia's posters hung all around the room. The one of Mr. Zizmore was directly over the stage area we'd created.

Wes had managed to borrow the elevated platform from the band department. He and the other teachers set up a microphone. And one of the parents who knows a lot about technical theater had set up great lights with colored gels borrowed from the drama department.

Somehow Wes had talked the custodian into letting us use the Sterno. He made some argument about how this was a private rather than a school function and so different rules applied. I'm not sure that was true, but it worked, so our hot food would stay hot.

"Isn't Claudia coming?" I asked Kristy, who stood with Sam by the soda table. We'd been a lot friendlier since our talk, but we hadn't gotten around to discussing the party.

She shook her head. "Mrs. Rodowsky called, looking for a last-minute sitter. Claudia said she didn't mind missing the party."

"But her artwork looks so great," I protested.

"For Claudia, the fun is in doing it," Kristy pointed out.

"Nice dress," Sam commented.

"Thanks," I answered. "I see a lot of kids from the high school are here."

"Yeah. I spread the word."

I noticed Robert looking uncomfortable, standing by himself in a corner. "Excuse me," I said to Kristy and Sam.

I crossed the room to Robert. "Hi, what's up?" I asked.

"Nothing, except I don't even know why I'm here."

"Because it's going to be fun," I told him. "Find Pete, hang out with him."

"Why? Don't you want to be with me?"

"Robert. I'll come by after I finish the eight trillion things I need to do."

He smiled at that. "I'll go find Pete."

I saw Ethan standing alone by the door and joined him. "I'm going to leave," he told me. "But I'll see you later. Your mom offered me a ride to the train station, since she was coming to pick you up after the party anyway."

"Good," I said. "Have fun."

"Sorry about this mix-up," he said.

"It's not a problem," I told him. "I'm sorry too."

He turned to go, then turned back to me. "Oh, and Stacey, you look great."

I smiled. "Thank you. See you later."

As I watched Ethan leave, Jeremy appeared alongside me. He wore a very serious expression. "I need to talk to you about something. Can we go out in the hall?"

"Okay." I followed him out.

"I know this is the wrong time to say all this, but I have to," he began.

"Say what?"

"Remember the other night after the movies, when you asked me if I wanted to break up?"

I nodded.

"I think you were right. We should."

I blinked hard, a little confused. "I didn't say we should break up. I wanted to know if *you* wanted to break up."

"Well, I do."

I breathed in sharply. "Why? Is it Claudia?" I asked.

"Yes and no."

"What does that mean?"

"I'm wondering whether I might like Claudia in a different way than I thought. But that isn't really why I want to break up. I'm not mad at you or anything. Really. I just see how you are with some of the other guys you've dated, and you seem to have more in common with them than with me."

I was about to say, *That's not true!* Only something stopped me. It *was* true.

Jeremy was great. I really liked him. But our relationship wasn't the same as the one I'd had with Ethan. Even Robert and I had been closer — right from the start — than I was with Jeremy.

And here was the main thing.

I wasn't particularly upset.

When your boyfriend breaks up with you, you should be at least a little upset. When Robert broke up with me, I cried. Sobbed!

But now, I just had a regretful feeling that Jeremy was probably right.

"If you really think it's for the best," I said.

"I hope we can still be friends."

I smiled to myself. Did I really need another ex-boyfriend friend?

Oh, well. It was better than being enemies.

"I hope so too," I said.

From outside, a horn honked.

"He's here!" I said to Jeremy. "We'd better get inside."

❀ Chapter 14

"Surprise!"

The lights flicked on and everyone shouted at once.

Mr. Zizmore stared, goggle-eyed. Obviously he was one hundred percent surprised.

Then — as planned — we all sang "For He's a Jolly Good Fellow!"

I noticed Toby signaling to me. He'd put on his jacket.

"I have to go," he said when I reached him. "I managed to call my family on our car phone and I told them where I am. They'll be here any minute."

"I'll walk you to the back door so we can watch for them," I offered. Toby was definitely not my dream guy, but he was my guest. And he'd been a good sport about the party.

"I found Mary Anne," he said as we walked down the hallway. "I told her my cousin Alex broke up with his girlfriend. He's available now. Since she's also free — who knows?"

"Isn't he in Pennsylvania?" I asked.

"Big deal. You and I got reacquainted. So. You'll come see me if you're ever in New Jersey, won't you?"

I knew I wouldn't. But it didn't seem necessary to say so. "I'll try," I fibbed.

We pulled the back door open and a cold blast made me jump back. "I see them," Toby told me.

He leaned forward. I knew he was expecting a kiss.

What the heck.

I pecked him lightly on the lips.

I guess it was good enough, because he smiled dreamily at me. "Until we meet again," he said dramatically.

I could only wave as he disappeared out the door. Then I headed back toward the cafeteria. By the water fountain, I met Wes. "Stacey, I got some good news today," he said. "Mr. Taylor called me."

Mr. Taylor is the principal of SMS. A call could only mean one thing.

"You got the job!" I cried.

"Yes!"

Wes Ellenberg — *gorgeous* Wes Ellenberg — was going to be my full-time math teacher! How would I ever concentrate? It was a good thing I'd already learned so much with Mr. Z., because I might not learn one more thing for the rest of the year. I'd be way too distracted.

We walked back to the party together. The music had begun to play. I glanced at Wes, wondering if maybe he'd ask me to dance, as he did once before.

That would have to wait, though.

Right now I had a speech to give.

I walked to the platform as Pete and Sam — one on each side — carried up the big, gleaming trophy we'd all chipped in to buy. On it shone a plaque that read: *To Mr. Zizmore, for inspiring SMS students to probe the infinite through the magic of numbers. With warm regards and thanks.*

I stepped up to the microphone and everyone quieted down.

"Surprise, Mr. Z.," I began. "This is the payback for all those surprise quizzes you've popped on us."

"Believe me, I'm surprised," he said, laughing.

"As everyone who knows me knows, Mr. Zizmore is my favorite teacher. This isn't to butter you up, Mr. Z., because unfortunately you won't be here for the next marking period. You're my favorite — and the favorite teacher of many, many students here — because you love what you do."

A ripple of applause ran through the room.

"There's a beauty in the order of number systems that can be as inspiring as music or great art," I continued. "And numbers can be mysterious, like the value of pi. No, not the cherry kind."

Everyone laughed at that.

"But I never saw the mystery and beauty of numbers until Mr. Zizmore's class. He inspired me to be more than good at math. Mr. Zizmore inspired me to *love* math. Thanks for that, Mr. Z. You've given me that gift, and it will be with me for the rest of my life."

Everyone started cheering.

To my surprise, tears sprang to my eyes.

I saw that Mr. Z.'s eyes looked bright too. But he was smiling. Beaming.

Pete and Sam walked the trophy to Mr. Zizmore. All around us, the applause and cheering continued.

At that moment— watching Mr. Z. receive his trophy — I knew that all the work had been worth it.

❋ Chapter 15

Toward the end of the party, Ethan showed up. I was glad to see him. "What are you doing back here?" I asked happily.

"I called your mom and said I'd meet her here so she wouldn't have to make an extra stop," he explained. "A guy I know dropped me off."

"Great," I said.

Ethan looked around anxiously. "I don't want to mess anything up for you, Stacey. I can just hang by myself until your mom comes."

"Don't worry," I said. "Jeremy and I broke up tonight. It doesn't matter."

His eyebrows lifted in surprise. The hint of a smile lifted one corner of his mouth. Then his expression became serious. "Are you upset?" he asked.

"I guess I should be. But I'm okay."

"Good," he said. "Was your teacher surprised?"

"Very. He just left. I think we made him extremely happy. He thanked me about a million times."

I looked around the lunchroom to see who was still there. Mary Anne was sitting at a table, talking to Robert. He seemed happier than when I'd talked to him earlier.

I spotted Jeremy at the far end of the room talking to Pete. Whatever they were saying seemed serious. I wondered if they were talking about our breakup tonight. At least Jeremy wasn't alone, brooding about it.

Sam and Kristy were with a group of people, all laughing and shouting about something.

Everyone seemed to be having a good time.

I yawned, suddenly realizing I was exhausted. "The cleanup committee will start knocking this down. We're all coming back tomorrow to finish up," I told Ethan. "Would you like to leave? We can wait for my mom outside."

"Sounds good," he agreed.

We found our jackets. I didn't even stop to say good-bye to anyone. If I started that, I'd be there for another half hour.

It was freezing outside. Ethan and I talked together happily despite it. Still, I was glad when Mom pulled up after only a five-minute wait.

As she drove to the station, I told her about the party and Ethan described the art exhibit.

"Why don't you go wait for the train with Ethan," Mom suggested when we arrived at the station.

"Thanks," I said, climbing out of the car.

Ethan thanked her too and we walked into the nearly empty station. Ethan had already bought his return ticket, so all we had to do was wait for the train to arrive.

"Stacey, I've been thinking about something since New Year's Day," he said.

"What?"

"I've really missed you."

"I've missed you too," I admitted.

"What would you think about spending a little more time together? What if I come up next week and take you for a tour of the Stoneybrook Art Museum? The exhibit is really good. I think you'd like it."

In the distance a train whistle sounded.

I put my hand on his. "That sounds like fun."

He smiled widely. "Great."

The whistle blew again. Louder.

"I'd better get down there," he said, suddenly seeming full of new energy. "I'll call you and set up the time. No more surprises."

"That's okay," I said. "Surprises are okay."

With a wave, he disappeared out the door.

It was funny, but I also had new energy all of a sudden.

I bounded out the station door to Mom's waiting car. Hopping into the seat beside her, I just grinned.

"How can you look so bright after the long, stressful day you've just had?" she asked.

I shrugged. She didn't know the half of it! "Being happy gives you energy, I guess."

As we pulled out of the lot, I gazed up at the stars. Maybe my stars and planets had lined up to bring back all my old boyfriends for an important reason — so I could pick the one who was really meant for me.

About the Author

ANN MATTHEWS MARTIN was born on August 12, 1955. She grew up in Princeton, NJ, with her parents and her younger sister, Jane.

Although Ann used to be a teacher and then an editor of children's books, she's now a full-time writer. She gets ideas for her books from many different places. Some are based on personal experiences. Others are based on childhood memories and feelings. Many are written about contemporary problems or events.

All of Ann's characters, even the members of the Baby-sitters Club, are made up. (So is Stoneybrook.) But many of her characters are based on real people. Sometimes Ann names her characters after people she knows; other times she chooses names she likes.

In addition to the Baby-sitters Club books, Ann Martin has written many other books for children. Her favorite is *Ten Kids, No Pets* because she loves big families and she loves animals. Her favorite BSC book is *Kristy's Big Day*. (Kristy is her favorite baby-sitter.)

Ann M. Martin now lives in New York with her cats, Gussie, Woody, and Willy, and her dog, Sadie. Her hobbies are reading, sewing, and needlework — especially making clothes for children.

Look for #7

CLAUDIA GETS HER GUY

Fifteen minutes later, my mom dropped me off in front of the main entrance to SMS. I bolted for my locker, hoping that Jeremy hadn't already passed by. His homeroom is in the same hall as my locker, so I see him nearly every morning.

I put my jacket away, then leaned casually against my locker, waiting. What would I say to him? How could I bring up the subject of his breakup with Stacey? I practiced a few possibilities in my mind. *So, I heard you broke up. How does it feel to be free at last? Looking for a new girlfriend, by any chance?*

Ugh. I decided it was better to be quiet and see what Jeremy had to say. I waited, excited and very, very nervous.

Finally, I spotted him walking down the hall in the middle of a crowd of boys. His hair looked shiny and clean, and he was wearing a red corduroy shirt that went beautifully with his eyes.

He saw me at the same time I saw him.

He smiled.

He gave me a little wave.

And he walked on by.

I felt one of the chopsticks fall out of my bun. And I felt my heart drop to the floor.

That wasn't what I'd expected.

All the time I had figured that now Jeremy and I would either be:

A) Friends or

B) More Than Friends.

I hadn't even considered possibility C):

Less Than Friends.